PUFFIN BOOKS

Sheltie to the Rescue

Make friends with

Sheltie

The little pony with the big heart

Sheltie is the lovable little Shetland pony with a big personality. He is cheeky, full of fun and has a heart of gold. His best friend and new owner is Emma, and together they have lots of exciting adventures.

Share Sheltie and Emma's adventures in

SHELTIE THE SHETLAND PONY
SHELTIE SAVES THE DAY
SHELTIE AND THE RUNAWAY
SHELTIE FINDS A FRIEND
SHELTIE IN DANGER

Peter Clover was born and went to school in London. He was a storyboard artist and illustrator before he began to put words to his pictures. He enjoys painting, travelling, cooking and keeping fit, and lives on the coast in Somerset.

Also by Peter Clover in Puffin

The Sheltie series:

Sheltie to
the Rescue

Peter Clover

PUFFIN BOOKS

PUFFIN BOOKS

Published by the Penguin Group
Penguin Books Ltd, 27 Wrights Lane, London W8 5TZ, England
Penguin Books USA Inc., 375 Hudson Street, New York, New York 10014, USA
Penguin Books Australia Ltd, Ringwood, Victoria, Australia
Penguin Books Canada Ltd, 10 Alcorn Avenue, Toronto, Ontario, Canada M4V 3B2
Penguin Books (NZ) Ltd, 182–190 Wairau Road, Auckland 10, New Zealand

Penguin Books Ltd, Registered Offices: Harmondsworth, Middlesex, England

First published 1997
5 7 9 10 8 6

Copyright © Working Partners Ltd, 1997
All rights reserved

Created by Working Partners Ltd, London W6 0HE

The moral right of the author/illustrator has been asserted

Filmset in 14/20 Palatino

Made and printed in England by Clays Ltd, St Ives plc

To David Honour

Chapter One

'Don't look so grumpy, Emma. It's supposed to be a holiday,' said Mum.

They were all sitting around the kitchen table looking at brochures: Mum, Dad, little Joshua and Emma.

Mum was looking at lovely pictures of pretty seaside holiday cottages. Dad was studying a large road map spread out across the table. And Joshua was trying to turn the pages of

1

the brochure that Mum was holding.

Emma just sat there with her hands folded in her lap, looking grumpy.

'Two whole weeks,' said Emma. 'It won't be much of a holiday if Sheltie can't come. And who will look after him while we're away?'

Dad looked up from the map, with a frown.

'We told you yesterday, Emma. Mrs Linney is going to pop over every day and feed Sheltie. Mrs Linney knows exactly what to do and how to look after him. There's no need to worry.'

'But it won't be the same,' said Emma. 'Sheltie's *my* pony now. I like looking after him. He'll think I've gone away and left him. He'll be miserable, just like me.'

'A fortnight isn't such a long time,' said Mum. She was beginning to look a little cross. 'Two weeks at the seaside, Emma. Just think of it.'

'I don't want to think about it,' said Emma. 'And I don't want to go. If Sheltie can't come with us then I'd rather stay at home, here in Little Applewood.'

Dad raised an eyebrow. He didn't say anything, but Emma could tell he was thinking hard. Mum ignored Emma and carried on flipping through the brochures.

'Look at this one. A tiny cottage right on top of the cliffs, overlooking the sea.'

Emma glanced at the picture of the little white cottage. But she was too busy thinking about poor Sheltie being left behind with no one to play with for fourteen whole days.

The next morning, Emma went into the paddock to give Sheltie his breakfast. She shovelled a scoop of pony mix into Sheltie's feed manger then gave him an extra tiny handful as a treat.

Sheltie stuck his head into the manger and gobbled up the pellets like a hoover. It always made Emma laugh when Sheltie did that. His head disappeared right inside the bin.

When Sheltie had finished, Emma took the hosepipe from the outside wall and filled his drinking trough.

Sheltie liked the water. He always

tried to drink it straight from the hose.
Emma aimed the hose at Sheltie and
gave him a squirt. Sheltie blew a loud
raspberry, then galloped playfully
around the paddock.

When Emma looked up she saw Mum and Dad standing by the paddock gate. They were both smiling. Joshua was there too, sitting across the top bar of the wooden fence. He was squirming like a little worm and Mum was holding on to him tightly.

Emma put the hose away and skipped over to the gate. She was ready for her own breakfast now and as they all sat round the kitchen table Mum told Emma some special news.

'Do you remember the holiday cottage we were looking at yesterday, Emma?' said Mum. 'The one on the cliff-top, overlooking the sea?'

Emma nodded and looked down at her shoes. She didn't want to think about going away on holiday and leaving Sheltie.

'Well, Emma,' said Dad, 'the cottage has a paddock at the back just like Sheltie's.'

'But Sheltie won't be in it, will he?' said Emma in a sulky voice. 'Poor Sheltie will be left behind all on his own!'

Dad raised an eyebrow at Mum then looked at Emma and smiled.

'Oh no he won't,' said Dad. 'I telephoned Mrs Linney this morning and she has a friend who is going to lend us a horse trailer. So now Sheltie can come away on holiday too.'

Emma's face lit up with a big smile and she clapped her hands with excitement.

'Do you really mean it, Dad? Yippee! Now it will be a real holiday for all of us.'

Chapter Two

Two days before the holiday, Dad collected the horse trailer. It looked like a little caravan on wheels. There was a big door at the back and a little window high up at the front for Sheltie to look out and see where he was going. The horse trailer was just the right size to take a little Shetland pony like Sheltie.

'It's just like a little house,' said Emma as she peered inside.

When Emma ran to the paddock and told Sheltie that he was coming on holiday, he became quite frisky and galloped around the little field tossing his head. She was certain he was as excited as she was.

The next morning Emma was busy helping Mum and Dad to pack their suitcases with everything they would need for two weeks by the seaside.

Then in the afternoon Emma helped Dad to load Sheltie's bags of pony mix and several bales of hay into the horse trailer. She hung Sheltie's bridle and saddle on the special hooks behind the door, then spread some straw across the floor.

Everything was ready for an early start the following day.

Bright and early on Friday morning
Dad tied the suitcases to the roof-rack
on top of the car. Emma put Sheltie's
head collar on him and led him up the
ramp into the horse trailer.

Sheltie gave a soft blow and looked

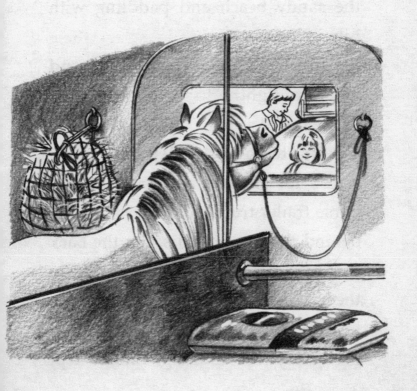

out of the little window. His bright eyes twinkled with excitement beneath his bushy mane.

Sheltie had never been away on holiday before, and Emma was looking forward to galloping along the sandy beach and paddling with him in the sea.

Little Joshua was excited too and held on tightly to his bucket and spade.

It was ten o'clock when they finally set off for Summerland Bay. Sheltie's horse trailer trundled along smoothly behind the car. Emma sat in the back seat next to the window. Mum sat in the back too with Joshua strapped into his special car seat.

As they drove along, Emma kept

looking behind to make sure the horse trailer was still there. Sometimes Emma could see the tip of Sheltie's nose poking through the trailer window. It was open slightly and Sheltie was sniffing the air. She knew he was enjoying every minute of the ride.

The journey took two hours, so it was midday when they finally arrived at their holiday cottage.

Cliff-top Cottage was much smaller than the cottage at Little Applewood. It was whitewashed, with a bright red door. On either side of the door were two little windows. Upstairs there were two bedrooms and a bathroom.

At the back of the cottage was a small paddock for Sheltie. The cottage

itself sat high on the cliff-top, with fields and meadows all around. The rolling heath ran to the edge of the cliff. And below, a footpath wound its way gently down to the sandy beach of Summerland Bay. It was a beautiful spot. The perfect place for a holiday cottage.

Chapter Three

Before they unloaded their suitcases
from the roof-rack, Dad helped Emma
to settle Sheltie into his paddock.

Sheltie's nostrils twitched as he
took in a deep breath of salty air.
Sheltie had never smelt the sea before.
It made him feel lively and he
galloped around his new paddock in a
full circle, shaking his long mane and
kicking his heels.

Sheltie seemed very happy. And Emma was delighted too.

Dad took the suitcases and carried them into the cottage. Then Emma helped Mum unpack all their things.

Dad made some sandwiches and a pot of tea, and everyone sat down outside at a little table in the garden. Emma and Joshua had fizzy drinks and looked out across the cliff-top at the sparkling sea beyond.

After lunch, they all went for a walk to explore the footpath which led down to the beach.

Sheltie didn't go. He was busy in his new paddock making friends with three stray ducks. Sheltie had rounded the ducks into a tight corner and stood with his head on one side listening to their noisy quacking.

Dad gave Joshua a piggyback ride as they all made their way slowly down the footpath to the beach.

At the end of the footpath there were twenty-eight wooden steps which led down on to the sand. Emma counted them all.

Once on the beach, Emma ran down towards the sea. She pulled off her shoes and socks and paddled in the foamy waves.

Further down along the beach some people were sitting on the sand: a man and a woman, and a young girl of Emma's age with dark, curly hair. When the girl saw Emma she got up and walked down to the sea.

Emma pulled a face. The girl was Alice Parker. She went to the same school as Emma. Emma didn't like Alice Parker very much. She was a show-off, and was always teasing Emma about Sheltie. Alice Parker had a pony too. Not a little Shetland pony like Sheltie, but a big brown one that shone like a conker.

Alice Parker was always saying that Sheltie had funny, stumpy legs and wasn't a proper pony at all. And she said that Emma looked stupid when she was riding him.

The two girls met at the water's edge.

'Hello, Alice,' said Emma, trying to be friendly.

Alice stuck her nose up in the air.

'Are you on holiday too?' asked Emma.

Alice didn't answer. She just turned and walked away.

Emma plodded back up the beach towards Mum, Dad and Joshua.

'Guess who's over there,' said Emma to Mum. She pointed along the beach with her finger.

'Is it someone you know?' asked Dad.

'It's Alice Parker from school,' said Emma. 'She's horrible.'

Mum looked over at Alice, who was now picking shells from the sand.

'She looks like a nice girl, Emma. Why don't you give her a chance? After all, if she's here on holiday too, it might be nice to have someone to play with.'

'Not Alice Parker,' said Emma. 'Besides, I've already tried.' She pulled a face. 'I'd much rather play with Joshua and Sheltie. Alice Parker calls Sheltie names. I'll never like her.'

'Maybe you'll change your mind in a day or two, Emma,' said Dad.

'I won't,' said Emma, feeling very

determined. She didn't like Alice Parker at school, and she wasn't going to like her on holiday. And that was that.

Chapter Four

The next day, Emma took Sheltie down to the beach. Sheltie was a tough little pony with a strong, steady walk. It was easy for him to take the winding footpath down to the sandy bay. But he couldn't manage the twenty-eight wooden steps, so everyone went the long way down.

Dad walked in front with Joshua sitting on his shoulders. Mum followed, carrying a picnic basket and towels for them all to sit on.

Emma led Sheltie by his reins. Sheltie plodded along, enjoying every minute of the sea breeze as it blew through his long shaggy mane. Overhead, the cries of the seagulls echoed in the blue sky. It was a beautiful summer's day.

Down on the sandy beach Emma climbed into Sheltie's saddle.

'Trot on, Sheltie.' Emma pressed with her heels and Sheltie trotted off across the bay, leaving a trail of little hoofprints in the soft golden sand.

At the water's edge, Sheltie stopped. He had never seen the sea before and he gazed out across the sparkling water. A crab scuttled by at his feet. Sheltie gave a loud blow and tossed his head as he pawed at the lapping waves.

Mum had laid the towels out on the sand and Joshua plonked himself down with his bucket and spade. Dad watched Emma and Sheltie trotting along in the surf.

'Don't go too far, Emma. Stay where we can see you,' called Dad.

Emma smiled back over her shoulder. 'We will,' she said. She rode Sheltie down to the end of the bay. Giant rocks sloped down from the cliffs into the sea. And there Summerland Bay came to an end.

There were little rock pools at the end of the beach. Emma dismounted to take a better look. Sheltie peered into a pool and saw his reflection in the water. Then he stuck his nose in and pulled out a long slimy string of seaweed. Sheltie gave the seaweed a good shake and Emma got sprayed with droplets of salty water.

Emma grabbed the other end of the seaweed. Sheltie held on fast and pulled. The seaweed tore apart and Emma sat down on the sand with a bump.

Sheltie pranced around with the seaweed hanging from his mouth. He did look funny – like a pony with a long green beard.

Emma laughed as she stood up and brushed the sand from her jeans. Just then, she noticed another pony and a rider coming along the beach, close to

the water's edge. It was Alice Parker.

'Oh no!' said Emma.

Alice Parker was riding a handsome white pony. Not a little Shetland pony like Sheltie, but a much bigger one.

Alice saw Emma and came trotting over. She brought the pony to a halt and gave a smug smile.

'Hello, Emma,' said Alice. 'I see

you've brought Stumpy on holiday with you.'

'His name's Sheltie,' said Emma. She was really cross. Emma found it hard to like Alice.

'This is Silver Lad,' said Alice. 'We're staying at Highcliff Farm. They have lots of ponies there. Proper ponies. It's a riding centre. I bet you wish you had a proper pony to ride, don't you, Emma?'

'No, I don't. I only like Sheltie. And anyway, he *is* a proper pony. He's a Shetland pony.'

Sheltie walked over to Silver Lad and looked up at the white pony. Their noses met and they sniffed each other and said hello.

'I'll give you a race,' said Alice,

smirking. 'Silver Lad against Stumpy.'

'I don't want to race,' frowned Emma. She climbed back up into Sheltie's saddle.

'You're scared,' said Alice. 'I bet Stumpy can't even run. His legs are too short!'

'Yes he can,' snapped Emma. 'Sheltie's really fast.'

'Come on then, scaredy-cat,' laughed Alice. 'Race you to the other end of the beach!'

Then Alice dug in her heels and Silver Lad took off at a canter along the stretch of beach.

Emma really didn't want to race. But Sheltie did.

Emma just squeezed gently with her heels and he was away in a flash.

Sheltie galloped after Silver Lad as fast as his little legs could carry him.

Emma hung on tightly to the reins as Sheltie raced along the shore. He wasn't fast enough though, and Silver Lad won the race easily.

'I told you so,' laughed Alice Parker. 'I told you that Stumpy couldn't run.'

Emma said nothing. She was upset and angry. It wasn't fair. Sheltie only had little legs. Emma turned Sheltie around and walked him back along the beach.

She leaned forward and patted Sheltie's neck.

'Never mind, boy. You're better than Silver Lad any day!'

Chapter Five

The next morning, Emma didn't want to go down to the beach. She didn't want to meet Alice Parker again.

Instead, she asked Mum if she could ride Sheltie out over the downs. There was a bridle path that led off from their holiday cottage across the heathland.

Mum said it was OK as long as Emma kept away from the cliff-top and didn't go too far. Emma promised, then she and Sheltie set off on an adventure all on their own.

Emma rode Sheltie along the bridle path. It was nice and quiet up there. Sheep were grazing peacefully all across the downs. The best thing of all though, was that there was no Alice Parker.

Emma had been riding for about ten minutes when she noticed something glinting up ahead, just off the bridle path.

What's that funny looking thing? thought Emma. It was a metal bar gleaming between the gorse bushes and the heather. Emma dismounted and walked up to it.

The shiny bar turned out to be the

handle of a silver shopping trolley. Just like the ones they have in supermarkets.

What's that doing up here in the middle of nowhere? Emma thought.

Sheltie saw it too and trotted over to investigate. There were some white things sticking out between the bars of the trolley. They were feathers. Three long white feathers. Emma pulled them free and Sheltie tried to eat them.

'I wonder what kind of bird these came from?' Emma said to Sheltie. Sheltie put his head over to one side, listening carefully.

The feathers were very long.

'It must have been a big bird,' said Emma. 'A seagull perhaps!' She looked up at the sky. Sheltie looked up too. But the feathers seemed far too long for a seagull.

'Maybe it was an ostrich,' laughed Emma. She held the feathers together at one end like a fan and climbed back into the saddle.

They continued on their way across the downs. Emma pretended that she was a lost princess riding across the desert. She waved the fan and tickled Sheltie's ears. Sheltie swished his tail and blew a loud raspberry.

Half an hour later, when Emma and Sheltie came back along the bridle path, the supermarket trolley had gone.

How strange! thought Emma. Who on earth would have pushed a trolley

all the way up to the downs and then taken it away again? Emma was puzzled by the mystery.

They continued slowly back to the holiday cottage, following the path round the curve of a hill.

Suddenly, the narrow track dipped

sharply and Sheltie stumbled. When Sheltie started to walk again he was limping.

'Oh, poor Sheltie,' said Emma. She slid out of the saddle. 'Have you hurt your leg?' Sheltie lowered his head and stood holding his front hoof up off the ground. Emma felt his leg and looked at his hoof, but she couldn't see anything. She was really worried.

'You poor thing. Can you manage the rest of the way? It's not far now.'

Sheltie hobbled forwards, limping, as Emma led with the reins. They walked very slowly. Each time Sheltie's foot touched the ground he lifted it again very quickly.

Emma led Sheltie off the hard stony track and on to the soft grass. She hoped it was nothing serious. She wanted to get Sheltie back to the cottage as quickly as possible.

'If we cut across here, it won't be so far,' said Emma. They walked away from the winding bridle path. Sheltie limped on as best as he could.

Suddenly the grass ahead sloped away down into a big dip, like a giant basin in the landscape. They stood on its rim overlooking the roof of an old tumbledown cottage.

Maybe someone there could help, thought Emma.

Chapter Six

A little path wound its way down to the front door. Dandelions grew up all over the front step. It looked as though nobody lived in the cottage after all.

Then Emma saw the supermarket trolley parked outside and her eyes grew wide.

While Emma was staring, an old woman came out of the cottage. She held a ginger cat cradled in her arms like a baby.

'Hello,' called the old woman. She was dressed in a funny old raincoat tied at the waist with string. But she had a nice friendly smile.

'Hello,' said Emma.

'Have you come to see the animals?' asked the old woman.

Emma didn't quite know what to say.

'We're staying at Cliff-top Cottage,' she said. 'We're on holiday. This is Sheltie. He's hurt his leg and he can't walk properly.'

Sheltie shook his mane and whinnied softly. He stood with his head low, looking at his hoof.

'Better bring him down and let me

have a look at him then,' said the old woman. Her voice sounded kind and caring.

Emma led Sheltie down the winding path into the little front garden. The old woman put the cat down and came over. She felt Sheltie's leg, then lifted his hoof and had a good look at it.

'He's got a stone caught under his shoe,' said the old woman. 'I'll fix that. Your little pony will soon be as good as new.'

She went into the cottage and came out holding a hoof pick. Sheltie stood very still and let the old woman lift his leg. She then carefully removed the stone from his hoof.

'There, that's better, isn't it, Sheltie?'

Sheltie could put his foot down comfortably now.

'What a nice friendly pony.' The woman gave Sheltie a hard pat.

Emma liked the old woman. Her name was Mary. She looked funny, but she was very kind.

Mary lived in the cottage by herself and cared for all kinds of sick and injured animals. People brought them to the cottage for Mary to look after. And sometimes the animals came all by themselves.

Mary asked Emma if she would like to see the animals. Emma said she would, but thought it best if she asked Mum and Dad first.

It wasn't far to Cliff-top Cottage. Luckily Sheltie's hoof was as good as new and he trotted back happily along the bridle path.

In no time at all Mum and Dad got to hear all about Mary and how she had helped Sheltie. Emma also told them about Mary's animal hospital and asked if she could go back and see all the animals. Dad said he would go with her that afternoon.

After lunch Emma plopped the saddle on to Sheltie's back and tightened the leather girth around his fat tummy. Then she slipped on the bridle and mounted.

Mum and Joshua stood outside the cottage and watched as Emma, Sheltie and Dad made their way along the bridle path and out over the heathland.

'Bye-bye,' gurgled Joshua, who was just learning to talk.

'Be back at five in time for tea, you two!' Mum called after them. Emma smiled and gave a wave. Sheltie blew a raspberry and made Dad laugh.

*

Mary came out of the cottage when she heard Emma, Sheltie and Dad approaching.

'Hello,' Dad called cheerfully when he saw Mary.

Mary greeted them with a warm smile. 'Hello, Emma. Hello, Sheltie.'

Sheltie shook his head and tossed his mane.

Dad introduced himself, then Mary took them behind the cottage to see the animal hospital and to meet all her patients.

There was Harold, a hairy goat with a gammy leg, and Doris, an old seaside donkey that nobody wanted any more. Poor Doris was blind in one eye. Harold and Doris both lived in a little field which backed on to the cottage.

A fox that had been hit by a car lay on some straw in a wire cage.

'He's still a bit poorly,' said Mary. 'But he's going to be fine.'

There was a badger too, that had hurt its foot, several rabbits, a family of hedgehogs, two seagulls and an owl.

And in a wooden pen at the far end of Mary's hospital was a beautiful white swan.

'This is Snowy,' said Mary. 'He flew into some overhead wires and damaged his wing. It's mended now but he won't be able to fly for a while. Every day I put Snowy in the supermarket trolley and take him up to Hollow's Pond on the heath. He has a little swim and then I bring him

45

back. He's ever so gentle. When he can fly and look after himself I'll release him back into the wild.'

Now Emma knew where those long white feathers came from!

Mary told Emma and Dad how all

the animals would eventually go back to their homes when they were well enough. All except Harold and Doris. They were like family to Mary.

'If you like, Emma,' said Mary, 'tomorrow you can come with me to Hollow's Pond and watch Snowy swim. Would that be all right?'

'Oh, can I please, Dad?' said Emma.

Dad said she could. He liked Mary and thought she was a nice, kind old lady.

'And can Sheltie come too?' asked Emma.

'Of course,' said Mary.

Sheltie threw back his head and let out the loudest snort Emma had ever heard. Sheltie liked Mary too.

Chapter Seven

In the morning, Mum gave Emma two small fruit pies which she had brought with her from Little Applewood. She popped them into a paper bag for Emma to take along to Mary.

Dad went with Emma and Sheltie as far as Mary's cottage, just to make sure that the visit to Hollow's Pond was still all right.

Mary was out in the back field,

hand-feeding Harold the goat and Doris the donkey with carrots and apple quarters. When they arrived, Emma rode Sheltie round to the back of the cottage and right up to the fence.

Harold stood on his hind legs with his front hooves resting on the wooden rail and rubbed noses with Sheltie. Doris gave a low bray. It seemed to be her way of saying, 'Hello, Sheltie.'

Emma slipped out of the saddle and held Sheltie's reins. She smiled at Dad and handed Mary the fruit pies.

'What a lovely treat,' said Mary. 'I know who would like a piece of these.' Harold was doing a funny little dance and staring at the paper bag.

'You can have a piece later, you greedy goat,' laughed Mary.

She took the pies inside then went to Snowy's pen and gently lifted the swan up into her arms and put him in the trolley. Snowy seemed very tame and didn't mind Mary picking him up. Emma guessed that Snowy was looking forward to his morning swim.

Mary pushed the trolley and Dad watched Emma lead Sheltie alongside, up the narrow track which led away from the cottage.

'See you back at home,' said Dad.

Hollow's Pond wasn't very far. It was near the spot where Emma had first seen the supermarket trolley hidden in the bushes.

Mary lifted Snowy from the trolley

and carried him over a grassy hump
and down into a shallow dip on the
other side. In the hollow was a little
secret pond, hidden away from the
rest of the heath. You would never

have guessed that there was a pond there at all if you didn't know about it.

Long reeds grew all around the pond at the water's edge. Mary lowered Snowy to the ground and the swan waddled into the shallow water. He waggled his tail feathers and swam out to the middle of the pond.

Emma and Sheltie watched as Snowy glided gracefully across the water. He looked so beautiful. No one would ever have known that he had damaged his wing.

Sheltie grazed on the grassy bank, nibbling at a patch of dandelions, while Emma and Mary watched the swan.

After a while, Mary took some lettuce leaves from her pocket and dipped them in the water. Snowy glided over and waddled up on to the bank. He took the leaves and then shook his tail feathers. Mary picked him up and carried him back to the trolley.

'Before we go back,' said Mary, 'I'll show you another secret.'

'Another secret!' chirped Emma.

Sheltie pricked up his ears.

Mary told Emma about a pair of peregrine falcons which were nesting on a ledge on the cliff-face.

'They are very rare birds,' Mary said. 'And they're hatching two eggs. Come along, I'll show you.'

Chapter Eight

They pushed the trolley across to the cliff-top.

Emma tethered Sheltie and followed Mary to the edge of the cliff.

Mary held Emma's hand and they stood looking down the steep cliff-face.

'Be careful now, Emma,' said Mary. 'Don't stand too near.'

They peered over the edge. Below,

halfway down, a narrow path hugged the cliff-face. And beyond that, a long, long way down, was the beach. Emma could see Alice Parker down there riding Silver Lad along the shore.

Emma noticed how far down the beach was. Her legs felt wobbly. Alice Parker looked *so* tiny, like a small round pebble.

Mary pointed to a ledge. Two

falcons were perched on the rocky lip. One bird was sitting on a nest.

'The eggs should hatch soon,' said Mary. 'And we should see two fluffy chicks before the week is out.'

'Oh,' cooed Emma. 'That would be wonderful.'

Then Emma looked at the cliff path.

'Where does that lead to?' she asked.

'The cliff path runs right down to the beach,' said Mary. 'But it's very dangerous. Don't *you* ever go down there,' she added.

'I won't,' said Emma. The path looked far too dangerous. Although there were some wider bits, it was mainly very narrow.

*

Emma was back at Cliff-top Cottage in time for lunch. Dad had made some salad rolls and they all sat outside in the garden to eat them. Then they had some delicious strawberry ice-cream.

Emma was so excited. She told Mum and Dad all about Snowy and how graceful he was when he swam. And she told them about the peregrine falcons and the nest.

'You were very lucky to see a pair nesting like that,' said Dad. 'You must be careful not to disturb them.'

Emma smiled. 'Don't worry, they're too far away.' She was having such a wonderful holiday.

That afternoon, they left Sheltie in the paddock, grazing in the summer sunshine, and went for a drive to the little quay around the next bay.

Colourful fishing boats bobbed up and down in the harbour. Emma's family walked along the thin strip of beach collecting shells. Emma found a piece of driftwood in the shape of a fish. Mum said she would help Emma to paint it. Emma wanted to give the driftwood to Mary as a present when they left.

Mum said she would like to meet Mary and pay her animal hospital a visit. She wanted Joshua to see Snowy and the animals. And Dad was hoping to see the two falcons.

When they arrived back at Cliff-top Cottage Emma decided to ride Sheltie across the heathland. She said she would pop in to see Mary and ask if it would be all right to bring all the family over the following day.

Mary's cottage was only ten minutes' ride away, but when Emma and Sheltie got there Mary was nowhere to be seen. All the animals were there. Harold and Doris were in the field. The trolley was there, and so was Snowy in his little pen. But there was no sign of Mary.

Emma thought that perhaps the old lady had gone to watch the falcons. She turned Sheltie and rode over to the cliff-top. Mary wasn't there either.

Emma stood up in the stirrups and looked around. She couldn't see the old lady anywhere.

Sheltie raised his head and sniffed
at the air. Then he blew a loud snort.

Emma slid off the saddle and left
Sheltie to nibble at the grass as he

usually did. But Sheltie was more interested in the edge of the cliff-top. He trotted over to the rocky edge and gave several more noisy snorts. Then Sheltie pawed at the rock with his hoof.

What is he so upset about? thought Emma. She went over to take a look. Emma stood as near to the edge of the cliff as she dared and peered over. She gasped in horror at what she saw.

There below, on the narrow cliff path, were Alice Parker and Silver Lad!

Chapter Nine

Emma could see that Alice had taken Silver Lad up the cliff path from the beach and now they were stuck. The poor pony was terrified and had refused to go any further.

Alice stood beside Silver Lad on the narrow path, unable to move. She looked very scared.

It was a long way down to the beach and the cliff-face was very steep. Alice clung on to Silver Lad's reins and looked up at Emma, pressing herself against the cliff-wall. She was so pleased to see Emma that she burst into tears.

'Please help!' sobbed Alice. 'We're stuck. Silver Lad won't move. He won't go forward and I daren't turn him.' Alice was really very frightened. Her face was almost white.

'Just stay there and keep still,' said Emma. 'Don't move at all. I'll take Sheltie and fetch help.'

Emma thought she would ride back to Mary's cottage to see if she had come home. But then she thought she could gallop back quickly and fetch Dad. He'd know what to do.

But before Emma could do anything, Sheltie had gone to the rescue. He had seen where the cliff path began between a gap in two big rocks and was already on his way.

'Sheltie!' called Emma. 'Come back!'

But it seemed as though Sheltie knew that Alice and Silver Lad were in serious trouble. He carefully stepped on to the narrow path.

It was very steep at first, but then the path levelled out a bit and became a little wider.

Emma followed behind Sheltie. She was scared, but took the path slowly, one step at a time.

'Be careful,' cried Alice from below.

Silver Lad let out a pitiful whinny.

Sheltie was a very brave pony. And being small, with a strong steady walk, he was able to tread the path easily. Emma walked close behind, keeping her back to the cliff-wall and moving along sideways, trying not to look down.

The wind whipped her cheeks and the waves crashed on to the beach below. Emma bit her bottom lip and called to Alice.

'We're coming! Don't be scared,' Emma shouted, even though she was scared herself.

Sheltie carried on. He was very sure-footed and didn't seem to be afraid. He seemed determined to rescue Alice and Silver Lad.

As he moved forward, Emma drew
in her breath and stood watching, as
still as a statue. She could see that the
pathway just in front of Sheltie was
dangerously narrow. And one small
part was missing where the rock had
crumbled away.

Emma gasped as Sheltie nearly put his foot over the edge.

'Sheltie, please be careful,' cried Emma.

Sheltie looked round and shook his head with a loud snort as if to say, 'I'm all right, Emma.'

Chapter Ten

With only a few metres left to go, Sheltie suddenly heard a voice calling from above. He looked up. It was Mary. The old woman looked very worried as she peered down at Emma and Sheltie from the cliff-top above them.

'Take care, Emma,' called Mary. 'Don't make any sudden movements, and stay close to the cliff-face. I'm coming to get you.'

Mary began to climb down on to the path. Emma edged her way back and took Mary's outstretched hand.

From the cliff-top they could see that Sheltie had reached Alice. He stood on a wider piece of path just in front of Silver Lad and turned around.

Emma called down to Alice. 'Reach forward and take hold of Sheltie's tail!'

Alice was so frightened she could hardly move. Sheltie gave a soft snort.

Mary spoke softly to Alice. 'Move forward slowly,' she said. 'Look straight ahead. Hold on tightly to Sheltie's tail and lead the other pony.'

Alice took Silver Lad's reins, then holding on to Sheltie's tail they began to move slowly.

Seeing Sheltie seemed to give Silver Lad the courage he needed to move forward. The frightened pony trod carefully and followed Alice and Sheltie.

When Sheltie reached the narrowest part where the path had crumbled away, Emma called down gently to Sheltie. 'Go on, boy. Just a little further.'

Sheltie looked up and answered with a soft blow. He carefully stepped past the crumbling edge and led Alice on. But Silver Lad was too frightened. The pony stopped again and Alice had to let go of his rein.

Mary went down on to the path again and called Sheltie forward. She reached out for his rein and helped

him along the last bit, up on to the
cliff-top.

When they were safely away from
the path, Alice burst into tears.

'I was so scared,' she sobbed, and

71

threw her arms around Emma, giving her a big hug.

Before anyone had time to blink, Sheltie went back down on to the path. Silver Lad was still stuck. The poor pony was terrified and all on his own.

Sheltie stood at the start of the path and made funny pony noises. Soft snorts and whinnies that called to Silver Lad as if to say, 'Come on, you're nearly there.'

Sheltie nodded his head and Silver Lad moved slowly forward on his own. He trod with care and began walking towards Sheltie.

Mary, Emma and Alice held their breath as Sheltie and Silver Lad clambered up on to the cliff-top.

Sheltie nuzzled up to Silver Lad. The poor pony was shaking from head to hoof.

Mary stroked the pony's muzzle and spoke softly to him. Her voice soon calmed Silver Lad down.

Emma went over to Sheltie and put her arms around his neck.

'Oh, Sheltie. You were so brave.'

Sheltie gave a loud snort, then pushed his soft velvet muzzle against Emma's cheek and blew hot air down the side of her neck.

'You have a very special pony there, Emma,' said Alice.

'I know,' said Emma. 'I don't know what would have happened if it wasn't for Sheltie.'

Alice had stopped crying. 'I'm so

very sorry I've been horrible to you and Sheltie, Emma.' Her eyes were all red and puffy. She looked very embarrassed. 'I can't thank you and Sheltie enough for saving us.' Alice looked down at her shoes.

'We had better get you two back home,' said Mary.

They led the two ponies back to Mary's cottage and the old woman telephoned Highcliff Farm, where Alice was staying.

Alice's mother and father drove up with a man from the riding school to collect Alice and Silver Lad. They were both very grateful to Emma and said they would like to send her a little present as a special thank you when they got back to Little Applewood.

Emma rode back to Cliff-top Cottage on Sheltie to tell Mum and Dad all about their adventure.

'What a silly girl Alice was,' said Mum. 'Fancy taking a pony up such a dangerous path.'

Although Mum and Dad said that Emma should never have attempted to rescue Alice alone, they understood that Sheltie had taken the lead. Emma and Sheltie had been very brave. Mum and Dad were so proud of their daughter and her little pony.

'It's a good job Sheltie came along with us on holiday after all, isn't it, Mum?' said Emma.

Chapter Eleven

The rest of the holiday passed by very quickly. Emma didn't see Alice Parker on the beach again. Not even once. Apart from a few other families they had the golden sands all to themselves.

Each day Emma rode Sheltie along the shore. Sheltie was excited by the smell of the sea and the soft ground beneath his feet. He pranced about on the sand and Emma raced him along the stretch of beach, sending the seagulls screaming and soaring over their heads. It was wonderful.

Every day they also went to visit Mary and the animals.

By the following week the fox was up and walking and Mary said that in another week he would be strong enough to be released back into the wild.

The badger was getting better too. And Snowy could now spread his wings and flap them with ease. He still couldn't fly yet, but Mary said that he soon would.

Emma and Sheltie also went with Mary to Hollow's Pond and watched the swan take his daily swim.

'Just think,' said Emma, 'when I'm back home, Snowy's wing will be as good as new and he'll be flying free. Do you think he will remember us?'

'I'm sure he will,' smiled Mary. 'How could anyone forget you and Sheltie?'

Sheltie blew a raspberry and shook his mane.

They strolled to the edge of the cliff-top and watched the two falcons. The hen-bird sat on the nest and Mary said that the eggs should be hatching very soon.

On their last full day in Summerland Bay, Emma and Sheltie took Mum, Dad and Joshua to visit Mary. They saw all the animals and strolled up to the cliff-top to see the falcons.

The two chicks had finally hatched! They sat in the nest and poked their fluffy little heads out from beneath their mother's wing.

Dad looked through his binoculars as the cock-bird brought food to the nest.

'Birdy!' laughed Joshua.

'This has been the best holiday ever,' said Emma.

Before they left, Emma gave Mary the painted driftwood fish that Mum had helped her to decorate as a present. It was beautifully painted, with colourful scales, eyes and fins.

'I shall treasure it always,' said Mary with a little tear in the corner of her eye. She gave Emma a big hug.

Sheltie nuzzled Mary's cheek with his nose and gave her face a lick.

Chapter Twelve

The next morning the holiday finally came to an end.

Emma helped Mum to pack up all their things and Dad tied the cases on to the roof-rack on top of the car.

When everything was ready Emma felt very sad to leave the holiday cottage. Sheltie was settled safely in the horse trailer and they climbed into the car and set off for home.

Mary had come to the cottage to say goodbye and Emma and Joshua waved as the car pulled away and disappeared down the track to join the main road.

'I'll write to you from Little Applewood,' Emma called through the open window.

Mary smiled and waved until the car was out of sight.

At home, Emma told her best friend Sally all about her wonderful holiday. Sally had ridden over on Minnow as soon as she knew they were back. Sheltie liked Minnow and his eyes twinkled with delight when he saw him.

Emma and Sally went riding

together all over the countryside around Little Applewood. And when they rode up to Horseshoe Pond they sat and talked about Mary, Snowy the swan and all the animals in Mary's hospital.

Emma wrote to Mary, and very soon afterwards a letter arrived for Emma from Summerland Bay. Inside the envelope along with Mary's reply was a cutting from the local newspaper. 'DARING CLIFF-TOP RESCUE' was the heading on the page.

Mum read the article aloud:

'While on holiday at Summerland Bay, brave Emma Matthews and her fearless Shetland pony, Sheltie, came to the rescue of Alice Parker and her pony Silver Lad when they became trapped on the cliff path overlooking the sea. Without a thought for his own safety, brave Sheltie climbed down on to the narrow cliff path and with Emma's help led the trapped girl and her pony to safety in a daring rescue. Emma Matthews and Sheltie live in Little Applewood.'

'You and Sheltie are famous, Emma!' said Dad.

Emma blushed with pride. She was very pleased. 'But it was Sheltie really,' said Emma.

That morning a parcel had also arrived for Emma. It was from Mr and Mrs Parker. Emma ripped open the wrapping paper and inside was a

lovely book all about Shetland ponies.
There was also a note from Alice. It
read:

Dear Emma,

I hope you like the book Mummy and Daddy have sent you. I chose it for you myself because I know you like Shetlands. There are lots of pictures and some of the ponies look just like Sheltie. I think Sheltie is the bravest pony in the world and I hope we can all become friends.

Thank you again for coming to my rescue in Summerland Bay. See you in school.

Love, Alice

'What a nice letter,' said Mum.

Outside, Sheltie was waiting in the paddock for his breakfast. He was tossing his head and making the noises he always did when he was hungry. Sheltie's eyes shone brightly beneath his long bushy mane as he saw Emma looking out from the kitchen window.

'Sheltie really is the best pony ever, isn't he?' said Emma. 'What a lovely holiday we had. And Sheltie made it extra special, didn't he? Maybe Alice Parker isn't so bad after all.'

Then she trotted happily out to the paddock to give Sheltie his breakfast.

If you like making friends, fun, excitement
and adventure, then you'll love

The little pony with the big heart!

Sheltie is the lovable little Shetland pony with a big
personality. He is cheeky, full of fun and has a heart
of gold. His owner, Emma, knew that she and Sheltie
would be best friends as soon as she saw him. She
could tell that he thought so too by the way his
brown eyes twinkled beneath his big, bushy mane.
When Emma, her mum and dad and little brother,
Joshua, first moved to Little Applewood, she thought
that she might not like living there. But life is
never dull with Sheltie around. He is full of
mischief and he and Emma have lots of exciting
adventures together.

Share Sheltie and Emma's adventures in:

SHELTIE THE SHETLAND PONY
SHELTIE SAVES THE DAY
SHELTIE AND THE RUNAWAY
SHELTIE FINDS A FRIEND
SHELTIE IN DANGER

READ MORE IN PUFFIN

For children of all ages, Puffin represents quality and variety – the very best in publishing today around the world.

For complete information about books available from Puffin – and Penguin – and how to order them, contact us at the appropriate address below. Please note that for copyright reasons the selection of books varies from country to country.

On the worldwide web: www.puffin.co.uk

In the United Kingdom: Please write to *Dept. EP, Penguin Books Ltd, Bath Road, Harmondsworth, West Drayton, Middlesex UB7 0DA*

In the United States: Please write to *Consumer Sales, Penguin USA, P.O. Box 999, Dept. 17109, Bergenfield, New Jersey 07621-0120.* VISA and MasterCard holders call 1-800-253-6476 to order Penguin titles

In Canada: Please write to *Penguin Books Canada Ltd, 10 Alcorn Avenue, Suite 300, Toronto, Ontario M4V 3B2*

In Australia: Please write to *Penguin Books Australia Ltd, P.O. Box 257, Ringwood, Victoria 3134*

In New Zealand: Please write to *Penguin Books (NZ) Ltd, Private Bag 102902, North Shore Mail Centre, Auckland 10*

In India: Please write to *Penguin Books India Pvt Ltd, 706 Eros Apartments, 56 Nehru Place, New Delhi 110 019*

In the Netherlands: Please write to *Penguin Books Netherlands bv, Postbus 3507, NL-1001 AH Amsterdam*

In Germany: Please write to *Penguin Books Deutschland GmbH, Metzlerstrasse 26, 60594 Frankfurt am Main*

In Spain: Please write to *Penguin Books S. A., Bravo Murillo 19, 1° B, 28015 Madrid*

In Italy: Please write to *Penguin Italia s.r.l., Via Felice Casati 20, I–20124 Milano*

In France: Please write to *Penguin France S. A., 17 rue Lejeune, F–31000 Toulouse*

In Japan: Please write to *Penguin Books Japan, Ishikiribashi Building, 2–5–4, Suido, Bunkyo-ku, Tokyo 112*

In South Africa: Please write to *Longman Penguin Southern Africa (Pty) Ltd, Private Bag X08, Bertsham 2013*